WE'RE GOING ON A
LION HUNT

WE'RE GOING ON A
LION HUNT

For Chantelle and Sophie

ISBN 0-439-27842-2

Text copyright © 1999 by Macmillan Publishers Limited.
Illustrations copyright © 1999 by David Axtell.
All rights reserved.
Published by Scholastic Inc., 555 Broadway, New York, NY 10012,
by arrangement with Henry Holt and Company, Inc.
SCHOLASTIC and associated logos are trademarks and/or registered
trademarks of Scholastic Inc.

12 11 10 9 8 7 6 5   2 3 4 5 6/0

Printed in the U.S.A.   14

First Scholastic printing, February 2001

WE'RE GOING ON A
LION HUNT

David Axtell

SCHOLASTIC INC.

New York Toronto London Auckland Sydney
Mexico City New Delhi Hong Kong

We're going on a lion hunt.
We're going to catch a big one.
We're not scared.
Been there before.

We're going on a lion hunt.

We're going to catch a big one.

We're not scared.

Been there before.

Oh, no . . .

Long grass!

Can't go *over* it.

Can't go *under* it.

Can't go *around* it.

Have to go *through* it.

Swish, swash, swish, swash.

We're going on a lion hunt.

We're going to catch a big one.

We're not scared.

Been there before.

Oh, no . . .

A lake!

Can't go *over* it.

Can't go *under* it.

Can't go *around* it.

Have to go *through* it.

Splish, splash, splish, splash.

We're going on a lion hunt.

We're going to catch a big one.

We're not scared.

Been there before.

Oh, no . . .

A swamp!

Can't go *over* it.

Can't go *under* it.

Can't go *around* it.

Have to go *through* it.

Squish, squash, squish, squash.

We're going on a lion hunt.

We're going to catch a big one.

We're not scared.

Been there before.

Oh, no . . .

A Big Dark Cave!

Can't go *over* it.

Can't go *under* it.

Can't go *around* it.

Have to go *through* it.

In we go,
Tiptoe, tiptoe.

But **what's that?**

One shiny wet **nose!**

One big shaggy **mane!**

Four big furry **paws!**

It's a lion!

Back through the cave.

Back we go.

Tiptoe, tiptoe.

Back through the swamp.

Squish, squash, squish, squash.

Back through the lake.

Splish, splash, splish, splash.

Back through the long grass.

Swish, swash, swish, swash.

All the way home.

Slam the door—

CRASH!

We're all tired now.
Tired and sleepy.

Better catch a lion tomorrow instead!